THE CRAZY CASE OF
MISSING THUNDER

#1

THE CRAZY CASE OF MISSING THUNDER

by Tony Abbott

illustrated by Colleen Madden

EGMONT

New York   USA

EGMONT

We bring stories to life

First published by Egmont USA, 2012
443 Park Avenue South, Suite 806
New York, NY 10016

Text copyright © Tony Abbott, 2012
Illustrations copyright © Colleen Madden, 2012
All rights reserved

1 3 5 7 9 8 6 4 2

www.egmontusa.com
www.tonyabbottbooks.com
www.greenfrographics.com

Library of Congress Cataloging-in-Publication Data
Abbott, Tony.
The crazy case of missing Thunder / by Tony Abbott ;
illustrated by Colleen Madden.
p. cm. -- (Goofballs ; 1)
Summary: Long-time friends and fellow sleuths Jeff Bunter,
Brian Rooney, Mara Lubin, and Kelly Smitts, collectively known as
the Goofballs, investigate the disappearance of Thunder the pony
in their town of Badger Point.
ISBN 978-1-60684-164-8 (hardcover) -- ISBN 978-1-60684-340-6 (pbk.) --
ISBN 978-1-60684-298-0 (ebook) [1. Mystery and detective stories. 2. Lost
and found possessions--Fiction. 3. Ponies--Fiction. 4. Humorous stories.]
I. Madden, Colleen M., ill. II. Title.
PZ7.A1587Cr 2012
[Fic]--dc23
2011025294

Printed in the United States of America

Book design by Alison Chamberlain

To Janie and Lucy,
my beautifully goofy daughters.
—T.A.

Contents

1

The First Clue

My name is Jeff Bunter, and I'm a Goofball.

A Goofball private eye, in fact.

It all started when I was one year old.

I was at a fast food place with my family. I got bored and slid out of my high chair and under the table with a bag of French fries.

When I climbed back up, I had four extra-long fries stuck in my nose and ears.

I wiggled them all around.

"What a Goofball!" my dad said.

Then he frowned. "Oh no. I think I lost my wallet."

That's when I handed him his wallet.

I had discovered it on the floor under the table.

"A Goofball private eye!" my mom said.

The name stuck.

Luckily, the fries didn't. I ate them.

※ ※ ※

A few years later, we moved to Badger Point, where I met Brian Rooney.

The first time I ever saw Brian, he ran over to my house in his underwear.

"Hi, I'm Brian," he said.

"I'm Jeff," I said. "Where are your pants?"

"They blew off our clothesline," Brian said. "I tracked them with these."

He held up a pair of spaceman binoculars made out of two toilet paper rolls, a metal coat hanger, and some Band-Aids.

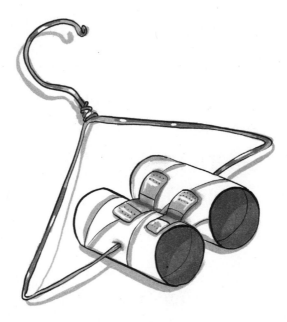

"You tracked your pants?" I said.

"To your house," he said.

Then he grabbed his pants from my bushes and put them on.

His head.

"What a Goofball!" I said.

Brian laughed and ran around my yard, waving his pants' legs.

My dog, Sparky, chased after him, barking and barking. Then Brian chased Sparky and barked even louder. Then Sparky slobbered on Brian's face. Then Brian yelled, "I'm going to puke!"

Then he became my best friend.

⚹ ⚹ ⚹

In first grade we met Mara Lubin and Kelly Smitts. They were firing squirt cheese into each other's faces.

"Hi, Cheese Cheeks!" I said.

Brian laughed. "Cheddar Cheese Cheeks!"

"Not just cheese," said Kelly, who had super-curly blond hair.

"Watch this," said Mara, who wore big green glasses and was as skinny as a stick.

They opened a cracker box and stuck little round crackers on each other's faces where the cheese was.

"Gross," said Brian. "I like it."

"There's a snack thief in our class," Kelly told us. "Some of my cheddar crackers are missing. And Mara's carrot sticks are gone."

"So we're going in disguise to catch him," said Mara.

Brian and I exchanged glances.

"Goofballs," I said.

7

"Major Goofballs," Brian said. "Want to team up?"

Mara nodded. And Kelly offered him a cracker off her face. "Come on," they said.

We tracked a tiny trail of crumbs to the classroom closet. We jerked open the closet door and discovered the culprit orange-handed.

"Joey Myers!" said Kelly. "With my cheddar crackers!"

"And my carrot sticks!" Mara said.

Then we saw the reason why. In Joey's lap sat Herbie, the classroom hamster, munching away.

"He was hungry!" said Joey, who suddenly crunched down on a carrot stick. "I guess I'm hungry, too."

"Cough up the evidence!" Kelly said.
Joey opened his mouth, and a half-
eaten carrot stick fell out.

Taking a small plastic bag from his pocket, Brian zipped up the evidence.

"Case closed!" I said.

Since then, the four of us have been inseparable. Hanging out. Doing stuff. And most of all being Goofballs.

Goofball private eyes.

Do you remember the Famous Riddle of the Exploding Rat Balloon? Or the Mystery of the Six-Fingered Ghost? Or the Episode of the Flying First Grader?

We solved all of those. Maybe I'll write about them someday. We had just solved the Unbelievable Affair of the Totally Incredible Pizza Disaster. It had been our biggest case yet, and it was tougher than an overdone crust.

Hot pizzas had been showing up mysteriously all over town. On the front steps at school. Floating in the pond at the park. Even folded up in the mayor's mailbox!

It went on for weeks. Pizza Palace was losing customers. Nobody got the pizzas they ordered. The restaurant was about to close down.

But then the four of us solved the mystery.

"Goofballs forever!" the pizza lovers in Badger Point had yelled. Everyone called us heroes. Luigi the pizza maker had put a photo of us on the wall of his restaurant. He even named a pizza after us.

You guessed it, the Goofball Pizza.

It has cheese, garlic, pineapple, and peanut butter. It's always fun to hear someone order us.

"A Goofball, please. With bananas!"

⁂

As soon as one case ends, we start looking for the next one.

Like now.

Whoosh! Whoosh! My feet were pumping hard on the pedals of my mountain bike.

Brian, Mara, Kelly, and I were going to meet up at the Badger Point Library.

Our cases usually finish up in the children's room at the library. That's because we often check out books to help us solve our mysteries. When the cases are solved, we meet to return our books.

It was a warm spring day, just before noon. Things were drying out after a big thunderstorm that morning.

Right.

Thunder.

That was the first clue.

Only I didn't know it at the time.

None of us did.

2

Suspicious Suspicions!

"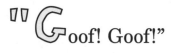oof! Goof!"

Sparky, my scruffy corgi puppy, is the official Goofdog. He barked while I biked to the Badger Point Public Library.

I knew Brian was skateboarding to the library on his homemade skateboard. Brian loves to invent and build crazy stuff. Most of it doesn't work. Most of it could *never* work.

But that just means he's a perfect Goofball.

Mara was probably running to the library, which isn't goofy at all. Running is how she stays so skinny, even though she eats pretty much everything in sight.

And Kelly? Kelly was most likely power walking.

She looks kind of nutty with her arms flying all around like an out-of-control windmill. Not to mention dangerous.

But she is never late anywhere.

"We're almost there, pal," I told Sparky as we rolled into the center of town.

Badger Point is small, but we have everything we need all mushed together. Across from the library is a movie theater. Next to that is Pizza Palace, where they name food after us. On the corner next to that is a flower shop. And up the street from that is the library again.

Ercch! I screeched to a stop and parked my bike. Sparky lay down next to it. He is good at guarding my stuff.

I gave him a few pats, then went inside.

I was early, and none of the Goofballs were there yet, so I went to the children's desk.

The librarian's name was Mrs. Bookman, which I thought was funny because she was neither a book nor a man. Her strawberry blond hair was piled up like a bunch of pink frosting.

Mmm. Frosting. That made me hungry.

So did the pizza books I put on Mrs. Bookman's desk.

There was *Crust or No Crust, That Is the Question.* Another was called *Hey, Dough!* The one I liked best was called *Saucy Sausage Sauce.* Try saying *that* five times fast!

"Mmm. These books make me hungry," Mrs. B. said.

"Me, too," I said. "But we'd better not eat them. We'll have to charge ourselves a fine."

Mrs. Bookman laughed. "Goofball!"

You could expect to see just about anything in the children's room. Story Time. Reader's Theater. Dress-Up-As-Your-Favorite-Character Day. But one thing you wouldn't expect to see was a big bag of dirt.

"What's with the dirt?" I asked.

I always ask questions. A private eye
has to ask lots of questions. It's how we
find out stuff.

Mrs. B. smiled. "The dirt is for the library's flower garden," she said.

It made sense. Gardens need dirt.

"You planted sunflowers last year," I said. "They grew really high. Crows were attracted to them. They were wild and noisy."

Mrs. Bookman laughed. "I even told them to mind their manners but they didn't listen. This year I planted tulips. But the thunderstorm this morning washed away some of the dirt. I'll be right back."

She got up from her desk and carried the bag of dirt through a door to the garden outside.

I saw thin green stalks with flowers blooming at the top.

A private eye has to notice everything. You never know what will turn out to be a clue.

To help me remember what I see, I write things down in a little notebook I have.

I call it my "cluebook."

I wrote a few things down now.

Thunderstorm this morning
Library garden
Dirt

As a detective, my job depends on being aware of every clue around me. That way, I always know what's happening.

I see everything that's going on.

And I'm never surprised.

By anything at all—

"Boo!" cried a voice behind my ear.

I nearly jumped out of my skin!

"Gotcha!" Brian said. "You were so clueless!"

Clueless.

That's the worst thing anyone can say to a private eye. But I was also a Goofball, so it was okay. "I knew it was you," I said.

"No way," said Brian. "I'm the best at creeping up behind people."

"You're creepy, all right," I said.

We both laughed.

Kelly and Mara raced in and slammed their pizza books on Mrs. B.'s desk.

"I won, I won, I won!" Mara cheered.

"That's okay. I wasn't racing," said
Kelly. "First one to the water fountain
wins!"

But Brian and I were the winners.
We cut them off and totally hogged the
water fountain.

Brian even tried to wash his feet in it, but Kelly threatened to wash his head instead, so he stopped.

"I wish we didn't have to find cases by accident," Mara said when we fell into the comfy chairs. "Real detectives get phone calls."

"Lots of people phoned about pizza," said Kelly. "That's how the Incredible Pizza Disaster got started."

"The *Totally* Incredible Pizza Disaster," I corrected her. "That's what I call it in my cluebook."

Mara sighed. "I can still smell the crust and all that gooey cheese—"

"Speaking of gooey," said a voice, "look, everybody—it's the *goo*-balls!"

We turned to see Joey Myers at the bookshelves. We had been in the same class ever since first grade, when we caught him snitching snacks. Now he was laughing so hard, he dropped his book. I saw the title. *All About Horses.*

Next to Joey was his friend Billy Carlson, who wore a faded baseball cap and shook silently when he laughed. "They think they're *pirate eyeballs*!" Billy said.

"The correct word is *Goofball*s," said Mara, squinting at the two boys through her glasses. "And we're not *pirate eyeballs*, we're *private eyes*."

But Joey and Billy ignored her and walked away, laughing and shaking.

"Just look at their ears," whispered Kelly when the boys had gone. "So guilty." She twisted her curly blond hair into ringlets. She always does that when she suspects someone or something. "I'll bet Joey and Billy committed the crime."

"Committed *what* crime?" Brian asked, while he was building a log cabin out of little yellow library pencils. "We don't even have a case yet."

"I'm pretty sure they did it anyway," said Kelly. "They seem pretty suspicious to me."

Suspicious is a good mystery word. It means not trusting something or someone you see.

And Kelly thinks pretty much everyone is suspicious. But I wouldn't trade her for anybody. It was Kelly who finally guessed the real reason that pizzas were appearing all over town. Maybe I'll tell you about it someday. But how did Kelly figure it out?

With that suspicious brain of hers.

Mrs. Bookman returned from the garden.

"Someday there will be a book about you kids in the mystery section," she said.

Mara sighed. "If we ever get a new case."

"We will," I said. "And I'm writing in my cluebook for exactly that purpose."

Kelly laughed. "For exactly what *porpoise?*"

"That'll be a *whale* of a story," Mara said.

"*Water* you talking about?" said Brian.

They all laughed at their silly puns.

"Goofballs," Mrs. B. said.

"With bananas," I added.

"Now I'm hungry," said Mara. "Can we eat? Maybe something with cheese?"

"Great idea," said Brian, setting the final pencil on his log cabin. "I'm actually working on a portable pizza machine so we can eat no matter where we are. I just haven't worked out all the bugs yet."

"Eew!" said Kelly. "Don't put bugs on my pizza!"

"Come on, guys," I said, slipping my cluebook into my jacket pocket. "Let's head up to my house."

Sparky led us as we biked, skateboarded, ran, and power walked back up the hill to my house for lunch. We skidded into the driveway together.

We tumbled right through the kitchen door.

Just in time.

To get . . . the phone call!

3

The Old Man

"It's for you, Jeff," my mom said when we all pushed into the kitchen. She held the phone out to me.

"Really?" I asked. "For me?" I glanced over at Brian, Mara, and Kelly. "Who could it be? All my friends are right here."

"And we don't even like you that much," Brian said. "Just kidding."

My mom shrugged. "Whoever it is, he's very polite. He asked for the original Goofball."

"That would be me," I said.

"Maybe he's got a case for us," Kelly whispered, and she crossed her fingers.

I took the phone. "Hello?" I said.

"Is this a Goofball?" said the voice. "The *original* Goofball?"

The voice was deep and scratchy. *An old man*, I thought.

"The absolute number one Goofball," I said, flipping open my cluebook. "Who is this?"

"You don't know me," the man said. "My name is Randall Crandall."

Odd name, I thought. *It rhymes.* I wrote it down.

Randall Crandall
Old man

"Go on, Mr. Crandall, sir," I said.

There was something like a cough at the other end of the line. Then he said, "I read in the newspaper about the Incredible Pizza Disaster."

"*Totally* Incredible, to be exact,"
I said.

"Everyone knows how you saved
that little restaurant," he said.
"Well, I have a case for you—"

"We'll take it!" I blurted out. Then
I caught myself. "I mean, please tell
me more."

"Something," said the voice. "Or . . .
someone . . . has disappeared. But I
can't tell you over the phone. Come
to my house. I live on Woodview
Avenue."

I added the name to my notebook.

Woodview Avenue

"What number on Woodview
Avenue?" I asked.

Mr. Crandall took a deep breath and
said, "Woodview Avenue is . . . my
driveway."

Click.

Mr. Randall Crandall hung up.

"Well?" said Brian, stuffing two paper napkins and a handful of toothpicks into the already bulging pockets of his cargo shorts.

"Well?" said Mara, staring through her glasses at the griddle on the counter.

"Well?" said Kelly. "What's the case?"

"This man wants us to find something," I said. "Or someone. I'm not exactly sure."

"What did he say?" asked Brian. "Some*thing* or some*one*?"

"Actually, he said both," I said, writing that in my cluebook, too.

"Sounds mysterious," said Mara.

"And suspicious," said Kelly, tugging on her curls. "The best mysteries are both."

When I told my mom where the place was, her mouth dropped open and she sat at the table. "That's the richest part of town, Jeff. I don't know *anyone* who lives up there."

I grinned. "Well, someone named Randall Crandall knows all about the Goofballs."

My mother nodded. "Well, there *was* that newspaper article *and* the photo in the restaurant and all those *flyers* you put up around town. I guess you *are* pretty famous."

"And also pretty famished," said Mara, still staring at the griddle. "Can we eat before we go?"

We did eat. Grilled cheese. With pineapple slices on the side. Mara was happy.

Twenty minutes later, we were all belted into my mom's SUV.

Brian sat next to Kelly but not next to me. I sat next to Mara but not next to Kelly. Mara sat next to Kelly but not next to Brian.

Mom didn't sit next to any of us because she was driving.

Which was good because our legs were too short to reach the gas pedal.

And Mom needed the gas pedal to drive us to Woodview Avenue.

And the house of Randall Crandall!

Rich, Rich, Rich!

We drove past the big woods and into the hills above Badger Point.

My mom made a right turn at the sign for Woodview Avenue and drove onto a long, winding road.

"Is this still the United States?" asked Brian, sticking his head out the car window.

"Will we have to stop for gas soon?" Kelly asked.

I looked back. "What a view! You can see the whole town from up here."

"I can see the library," said Mara. "Mrs. Bookman is watering her tulips."

"Sure, but take a look at that!" said Brian, sticking his head out the other window.

And there it was. A house bigger than any house I had ever seen.

My mom made a sound like, "*Ohhhhhh!*"

Two rows of tall trees lined the road leading up to the front door, which stood at the top of a long flight of steps.

My mom stopped the car and breathed sort of funny. "I'll stay here. I feel faint."

"Don't worry, Mom," I said. "We'll try not to get lost."

We walked to the foot of the staircase.

"Race you to the door!" said Mara.

"You're on!" I cried.

We all ran up the stairs for the door. At the last second, Kelly's arms went wild, Brian ducked sideways, Mara fell into me, and we all toppled into the front door.

At the exact moment it opened.

A super-tall man in a fancy black vest looked down at us.

"The Goofballs, I presume?" he said.

I tried to smile. "You presume correctly."

"I am Picksniff, Mr. Randall Crandall's butler," the man said. "Please walk this way."

But we couldn't walk that way.

Picksniff had super-long legs, and we had to run to keep up with him.

First, there was an entrance hall, then some stairs, then another hall, then five doors, then even more stairs.

"This is like a tour of the White House!" Mara said in awe.

"Actually, the Crandall residence is *bigger* than the White House," Picksniff said with a sniff as he hurried on.

"With more doors than a door store," Kelly said, counting them as we passed. "I bet there's something suspicious going on behind each one."

"Or maybe something delicious going on," whispered Mara.

Finally, after what seemed like half an hour, the butler stopped at a wide set of double doors.

"Wait in here," he said. "Mr. Crandall will be with you shortly."

He opened the doors for us, then hurried away on his long legs.

"Did that guy just call me 'Shorty'?" whispered Brian.

"No," said Mara, standing as tall as she could. "But I will. *Shorty!*"

Then we stepped inside the room.

And we all gasped with disbelief.

"Wow!" I said.

"It's bigger than our school!" Kelly said.

"It's bigger than Badger Point!" cried Mara.

"It's bigger than the world!" Brian said.

"Wow!" I said again.

Large paintings in gold frames were hung all over the walls like in a museum. In the middle of the floor sat a rug that could cover my entire yard. Around it were a dozen large, soft chairs. Behind them stood a fireplace you could park a truck in. I fumbled for my cluebook and wrote some more notes.

Rich, rich, rich!
Wow, wow, $ $ wow!

I know. Not the greatest notes. But they were the best I could think of.

Along one whole wall were shelves of books crammed tighter than socks in a sock drawer.

"You can discover a lot about a person from his books," said Kelly, power walking to the shelves. "And Randall Crandall has all the classics. Look. *The Molar Express.*"

"And *Charlotte's Website!*" Brian said.

"Plus my favorite," said Mara. *"The Magic School Bug—"*

"Welcome, Goofballs!"

We froze when we heard the voice. It was the deep voice I had heard on the phone. "Let me introduce myself. I am Randall Crandall."

The moment we turned away from the bookshelves, one of the huge chairs slowly swiveled around to face us.

A person was sitting in it.

I blinked when I saw him.

One of the notes in my cluebook was completely wrong.

Randall Crandall wasn't who I expected.

He wasn't who I expected . . . at all!

The Sound of Thunder

I stared at him. "But you're . . . you're . . ."

"A kid?" Randall Crandall said. "You *are* a good detective!"

He *was* a kid. He even looked as if he was in the same grade as us. Except that he was dressed like a principal. A principal who wears short pants!

"Is that a bow tie?" Brian asked.

"Are those diamonds on your socks?" asked Mara.

"I don't get it," I said. "The phone call. Your voice just now."

The boy stood and showed us a plastic cup with rubber bands stretched across the opening. He put it near his mouth.

"A simple trick," he said. "You press your lips on the rubber bands, lower your voice, and talk into the plastic cup like this. . . . "

The voice that came out next was raspy like an old man's. "I have heard you are the best."

"Except that you fooled me with a plastic cup!" I said.

"And it's super hard to fool a Goofball," Brian said, examining the cup closely.

Randall smiled. "That's exactly why I asked you to come. Please sit." He motioned to the big, soft chairs near the garage-size fireplace.

Before Randall could sit down, his butler rushed into the room and slid a chair under him.

Randall Crandall frowned. "Picksniff is always around. He's been with me for—"

"—ages and ages," said Picksniff.

"It's Pick's job to—"

"—help Master Randall with things," the butler added.

Randall leaned closer to us. "Including helping me finish my—"

"—sentences," said Picksniff.

"Watch this," Randall whispered to us, a twinkle in his eye. He stuck his nose into a vase of daffodils on a nearby table.

Then he squinched up his face as if he were going to sneeze.

"Ah-Ah-Ah—"

"—CHOO!" said Picksniff.

Randall's butler even sneezed for him!

"Please remove the flowers, Pick," Randall said, wiping his nose.

The butler frowned. "But they were delivered fresh this morning, sir."

·Randall nodded at Picksniff. "I know, but unless you want to be sneezing for me all day, you'd better take them. Suddenly, I seem to be allergic to daffodils."

"Yes, sir." Picksniff took the flowers away.

"So, what's this case all about?" I asked.

Randall's smile faded, and he looked out the window as if at something far away.

"Thunder," he said quietly.

I looked out the window, too. The sky was blue and clear. "I don't hear thunder outside."

"No, I mean my pony," Randall said.

"Your pony is outside?" Brian asked.

"No, I mean my pony's name is Thunder," Randall said. "And he's . . . missing."

"That's terrible," Mara said. "Jeff, your cluebook."

"Got it," I said.

Randall continued. "I always hear Thunder neighing this time of day. We would go riding, then we'd have lunch together. But now he's gone."

Thunder
Randall's pet pony
Gone

When I wrote those words, I understood what Randall had meant on the phone. He had said that some*thing* or some*one* had disappeared.

You could say that a pony was a thing, but to Randall his pony was some*one* he cared about. I added another clue.

Thunder friend

Kelly twirled her curls slowly. "Can you describe Thunder to us?"

"I can do better than that," Randall said, reaching for a picture of a short brown pony with furry ears and a long, wavy mane. "This is Thunder. He's ten hands high. That's forty inches."

"He's pretty small," said Brian. "With a name like Thunder, I expected a huge, monster-size horse."

Randall sighed. "That's our little
joke. Thunder's shy and not like his
name at all. He's terrified of storms,
and he doesn't like to travel. In fact, I
have to trick him to get him into his
trailer. He's rather a scaredy-cat."

Which is what I wrote.

Thunder afraid of thunder
Tricked into his trailer
Scaredy-cat

"I think we'll need some books about
ponies," said Mara.

Suddenly, I remembered the book
that Joey Myers had dropped that
morning at the library: *All About
Horses.*

Could Joey possibly be a suspect?
Kelly jumped from her chair and
stood up in the gigantic fireplace. She
looked like an actress standing on a
stage.

"One more question," she said. "When
exactly did you first notice Thunder
was missing?"

"This morning," said Randall softly. "His hoof prints just vanished behind the stable. How can we find him?"

I looked at my notes. "First, we take a look at the last place Thunder was. The stable."

But when I tried to get up from the chair, I couldn't. It was too squishy. Brian tried to get out and pull me up, but he was stuck, too.

"Kelly, help!" shouted Mara, reaching out for her but only managing to pull Kelly into her lap.

"Picksniff!" yelled Randall Crandall.

In two seconds, Picksniff was there, pulling us all safely to our feet.

"The butler did it!" Brian said.

"Butlers usually do," said Picksniff. "But not this time. I do hope you find Randall's pony."

Twenty seconds later, we were in Randall Crandall's personal elevator, heading down to Thunder's personal stable.

Hay!

The stable was a long white building as large as an airplane hangar.

"This is where Thunder lives," Randall said. "Or, it used to be."

When he pulled open the doors, a strong smell came floating out.

But it wasn't what you think.

The smell was sweet. Like a garden.

"Look," said Kelly, pointing to the ground inside the stable.

It was covered with yellow and purple flower petals.

"What happened?" I asked. "Why are there flowers all over the stable?"

"Thunder likes flowers," Randall said. "He likes their smell and even likes to eat them. He'll travel only if I fill his trailer full of flowers. He's still scared and won't move an inch once he's in the trailer, but the flowers comfort him when we travel. These flowers were delivered first thing this morning."

I wrote that down in my cluebook.

"In fact, there's only one food Thunder loves more than flowers," Randall said, "and it's one of the reasons I called you—"

"I see footsteps!" Brian interrupted.

He sank to his knees, dug into a pocket, and took out a bendy straw, a folding toothbrush, and three quarters. He brushed and fiddled and rolled them on the ground for a minute, then he looked up. "Just as I thought. *Recent* footsteps!"

"They're called foot*prints*," said Mara, staring at them through her big green glasses. "And they're definitely not grown-up prints. They're *kid* footprints!"

Randall blinked. "A lady was driving the flower truck this morning. The flower shop is called Petals and Buds. There were a couple of boys with her."

I frowned. "Petals and Buds? A couple of—"

Mara gasped. "Joey Myers's *mother* owns that flower shop!"

"And those weren't boys," Kelly said. "They were Joey and Billy! I knew it was them! Who are the pirate eyeballs *now*, I wonder?"

"Randall, when did you say Thunder vanished?" I asked, opening my cluebook.

"First thing this morning," Randall said.

"The same time the boys delivered the flowers!" Kelly said, twisting her curls into a knot.

I jotted it all in my cluebook and snapped it shut. "Next stop, the flower shop."

"Hey, that's a rhyme," said Brian.

"I do it all the time," I said.

"You're a poet," Mara said.

"I know it," I said.

Randall Crandall laughed. Then he frowned. "Please bring Thunder back safe and sound. I miss him."

I knew what he meant.

Just after we had moved to Badger Point, my dog, Sparky, had gotten lost.

I was afraid I'd never see his scruffy face again. When he had finally found his way home, I didn't stop hugging him for a long time.

Randall missed Thunder as much as I had missed Sparky.

"We'll find Thunder," I said. "There's no case we can't solve."

"There are plenty of math problems we can't solve," said Mara.

"And some mysteries of the universe," Kelly added.

"But no case," said Brian.

"I believe you," Randall said. "Thanks."

We all waved good-bye as the rich boy slowly walked back to his gigantic house.

"I bet he wants to come with us," Mara said.

Brian nodded. "I wonder if he wants to be a Goofball."

"I'm pretty sure everybody does," I said. "But first things first. Joey likes horses. He helped deliver flowers to Thunder this morning. Maybe he's graduated from hamster hider to horse rustler."

"Goofballs," said Mara, "it sounds like we have our first real suspect."

Kelly grinned. "My favorite word!"

7

Keep Your Plants On!

Five minutes later, my mom dropped us at the library. We rushed in to take out books about horses, but Mrs. Bookman said most of them were already checked out.

"By guess who?" said Kelly, staring straight across the street at Petals and Buds.

"Joey's not going to tell us much," I said when we gathered on the sidewalk. "He thinks we're *goo*balls."

"And he's probably still hungry because we didn't let him finish that carrot stick three years ago," Brian said. "That would make anyone mad."

"There's only one way to find out what we need to find out," Kelly said. "Our specialty."

Mara winked through her glasses. "Disguises!"

Carefully, the four of us snuck into the alley behind the shop. We found a big garbage can overflowing with leafy branches and broken blossoms.

"It smells good for garbage," Mara said.

"Just like Thunder's stable," Brian said.

"Joey is *so* guilty," said Kelly. "Come on."

Kelly and Mara began stuffing leaves and flowers into their belts and socks and sleeves.

Brian and I joined them. A minute later, there were four Goofball plants in the alley.

"I want to be a *hedge* when I grow up," Brian said with a chuckle.

"We'll have to *stick* close," said Mara.

"Just keep your *tulips* closed and let's go inside," Kelly said.

"Okay, but don't *leaf* me here!" I said.

On my signal, all four Goofball plants shuffled into the back of the shop as quietly as we could. We saw Joey and Billy watering plants with a garden hose.

Brian nudged my branch. "Joey's mom has a customer. Let's listen."

At the counter there was a woman holding a bunch of thin green stems without flowers.

I recognized her as our neighbor Mrs. Wilson.

"I ordered three dozen red tulips to be delivered this morning," Mrs. Wilson said. "But instead, look what I got!"

Joey's mother studied the stems without flowers. "I can't explain it. I'm very sorry."

Then she turned to Joey and Billy. "When you boys dropped off the flowers from the truck this morning, were they like this?"

"No," said Joey. "They were nice."

"Really nice," said Billy. "All flowery."

Mrs. Myers shook her head. "Well, did you notice *anything* strange?"

Joey looked at Billy.

Billy looked at Joey.

"He left the truck door open!" they both said, pointing at each other.

"What do you mean?" asked Mrs. Myers.

Joey grumbled. "When we stopped at Mrs. Wilson's house—"

"The back of the truck was open," Billy said. "Because somebody forgot to close it at that rich kid's house."

Randall Crandall's house, I thought. *Aha!*

"Joey forgot," Billy said.

"Billy forgot!" Joey said.

"It was raining so hard," Billy said, "we just jumped right back in the truck to stay dry."

"It was sunny by the time we got to Mrs. Wilson's house," Joey said. "That's when we noticed the truck door was still open."

Mrs. Myers turned back to Mrs. Wilson and sighed. "I'm terribly sorry the flowers got destroyed. We'll replace them, of course."

"Thank you," said Mrs. Wilson.

"As for you boys," Joey's mother said, "please continue watering while Mrs. Wilson and I choose new flowers. Those four big plants in the back seem very dry."

Four big plants? What four—

Uh-oh.

Mrs. Myers was pointing right at us!

Joey was pointing right at us, too.

With the garden hose!

Sploosh! Water spurted out like a tidal wave!

We got soaked from stems to blossoms!

I didn't have a butler to do my sneezing, so I had to do my own.

"Ah-Ah-Ah-Ah—" I started.

"That plant!" said Joey, backing far away from my shaking branches. "It's—it's—"

"—CHOO!" I exploded. It was the loudest sneeze in the history of sneezes.

"Whaaa—" Joey flew back right into Billy. The hose went wild and sprayed Billy from head to foot.

The last thing I saw as we raced out the back door was Billy swatting Joey with Mrs. Wilson's chewed-up flower stalks!

The Totally Incredible Solution

We charged down the alley, zigzagged behind the shops, dashed up the hill, and didn't stop until we got to my backyard.

We plopped down on a big flat rock to dry.

"That was close," said Kelly. "I'm so wet."

"That was closer than close," Mara
said. "I'm completely soaked."

"That was the closest!" said Brian.
"Even my insides are dripping! Too
bad we're not as close to finding
Thunder."

As I squeezed the water out of my wet socks, I read my cluebook from beginning to end. Two clues seemed especially important.

Thunderstorm this morning
Thunder afraid of thunder

Looking up the hill, I saw Mrs. Wilson's house. Looking down the hill, I saw the library garden. In between I saw my mom's garden. And I suddenly noticed that some of the flowers were eaten, just like at Mrs. Wilson's house.

My heart began to pound.

"Maybe we are close, after all," I said. "Really close."

"Do you know where Thunder is?"
Brian asked.

I jumped to my feet. "Yes! I've figured
it out!"

Kelly gasped. "Tell us everything!"

"No, that would take too long," said
Mara. "Just tell us what you figured
out."

I stood up on the flat rock like a
teacher in front of a class.

"We know that Thunder likes flowers and was last seen this morning. We also know that the flower truck made a delivery this morning. We *also* know that the storm was this morning."

"Boy, we know lots of stuff," Brian said. "We must be smart."

"Then answer this," I said. "What do we get when we put Thunder, the storm, and the flower truck together?"

"One of Brian's wacko inventions?" said Mara.

Kelly's hand shot up. "Oooh! Oooh! Me! Me!"

"Kelly?" I chose her like a teacher would.

She stood up, just like in class. "Well, what if Thunder went into the truck because he saw flowers but was too scared to leave because of the storm? If Joey and Billy didn't close the truck door, they never would have seen him in there!"

"Correct," I said with a smile.

"Now me!" said Mara, jumping up next to Kelly. "Randall said Thunder was scared even with the flowers in his trailer. What if he was too scared to eat the flowers, but by the time the truck got to Mrs. Wilson's, the storm was over, so he ran out?"

"And when the truck left," Brian said, jumping up next, "Thunder ate Mrs. Wilson's tulips."

"Wow!" said Kelly. "We really *are* smart."

I grinned. "Now, Brian. What was that question you asked before?"

"*Water* you talking about?"

"Not that question," I said.

"Is this still the United States?"

"Not that question," I said.

"I see footsteps!"

"That's not even a question," I said.

"Do you know where Thunder is?"

"That's the question!" I said. "And the answer is *right there!*" I pointed down the hill.

Brian pushed his hands into his bulging pockets and took out a tiny mirror, four bottle tops, three finger puppets, and the last page of a dictionary. Fiddling for a moment, he suddenly held what looked like a telescope!

He jumped. "I see Thunder! He's trotting right toward the library garden! He must have seen it from Mrs. Wilson's house and made his way down the hill right to it. He's on his way there right now!"

We ran inside my house and called Randall to meet us at the library. Then we raced down the hill to town, Sparky barking the whole way. "Goof! Goof!"

"Did you find Thunder?" Randall asked when he jumped out of his big white limousine in front of the library. "Where is he? Where's my Thunder?"

"Follow us," I said with a sly smile.

But when we arrived at the library garden, Thunder was nowhere in sight. So we waited. And we waited. And we waited some more.

No Thunder.

"Oh, no!" said Mara. "We didn't solve the case, after all!"

Suddenly, a shout echoed from across the street. "The Goofballs are completely ruined!"

"Boy, word spreads fast," said Kelly as everyone came running, even Joey and Billy.

Then we saw Luigi the pizza maker running across the street, waving his hands in the air. "The Goofball *pizzas* are ruined!" he cried.

The doors of Pizza Palace suddenly burst open, and out galloped a small brown pony. His nose was covered with globs of peanut butter and pineapple rings.

"That's a good disguise," said
Mara.

"That's Thunder!" yelled Randall
Crandall.

"He's heading for my flower shop!"
shouted Mrs. Myers. "Help!"

I turned to Randall. "Any ideas?"

Randall glanced at the library
garden and his face lit up. "A goofy
idea. Mrs. Bookman, may I?"

"Be my guest!" she said.

Randall snipped some flowers.
He stuffed them into his pockets.
He stuck them behind his ears.
He dangled them from his bow tie.
He slipped them in his hair.

Soon, he was a wiggly, wobbly,
walking flower bouquet.

"Thunder," he called. "Yoo-hoo, Thunder!"

The pony turned. His big brown eyes blinked. His furry ears twitched. He trotted right over and tugged a flower from behind Randall's ear. He chewed it all up.

"Oh, Thunder!" cried Randall. "I'm so glad the Goofballs found you!"

"Almost," Mara said.

"Sort of," said Brian.

"Not really," Kelly said.

"We were clueless," I said.

Randall laughed. "That's a goofy thing to say! I tried to tell you before. Thunder really likes flowers, but he *loves* pizza. Especially pizza with pineapples and peanut butter. If you hadn't solved the Pizza Disaster, there would be no Goofball pizza. With no Goofball pizza, Thunder might still be lost!"

"We *did* solve the case!" said Mara.

Kelly grinned. "The Case of Missing Thunder!" she said.

"The *Crazy* Case, to be exact," said Brian. "Jeff, write *that* in your cluebook."

"Goofballs forever!" everyone cheered.

Then Randall pulled a flower out of his hair and began to munch it. Using a napkin and two toothpicks from his pocket, Brian ate a flower, too.

Then Mara, Kelly, and I chomped some tulips. Even Mrs. Bookman, Mrs. Myers, Luigi the pizza maker, Sparky, and Joey and Billy munched flowers.

Proving what I always say.

Everybody wants to be a Goofball!

Meet the
GOOFBALLS!

Jeff Bunter is the #1, original Goofball. Jeff was born to solve mysteries. He is in charge of keeping track of clues in his ever-present cluebook. He says that a private eye has to notice everything—because you never know what might be a clue!

Brian Rooney is Jeff's best friend. He's an inventor who loves to build crazy things that don't always work but that look really cool and help the Goofballs solve mysteries.

Mara Lubin is as tall as a fashion model, as skinny as a rake handle, and wears giant green glasses. She's also a master of amazing disguises.

Kelly Smitts is as smart as a computer, but she doesn't look like one. Unless a computer is really short, really suspicious, and has curly yellow hair.

Sparky is the official Goofdog. He's Jeff's scruffy Pembroke Welsh corgi and he herds clues to help the Goofballs in every case. *Goof! Goof!*

Calling all GOOFBALLS!

☆ ▲ ☆ ▲ ☆

Laugh yourselves silly with the nuttiest team of detectives ever!

The Goofballs have solved
The Crazy Case of Missing Thunder.

Now follow them to Book 2—
The Startling Story of the Stolen Statue.

It's the Crime of the Century. Badger Point Elementary is gearing up for its 100th anniversary, but the statue of the first principal has gone missing.

And the Goofballs are on the case with Mara's kooky disguises, Brian's bizarre inventions that might or might not work, really silly puns that will twist your brain, grated cheese that will twist your stomach, and a ton of stuff that has nothing to do with anything!

With Sparky the Goofdog staying after school, the Goofballs comb the halls, climb the walls, and crawl into a piano for clues, but will they find the statue in time?